A Note from Michelle about
THE NOT-SO-GREAT OUTDOORS

Hi! I'm Michelle Tanner. I'm nine years old. And I'm about to go on the worst vacation ever.

My dad is taking me and my sisters camping. And you should see what he's packing—a billion kinds of cleaning supplies, an iron, and a book filled with gourmet recipes. Yuck!

Even worse, he signed me up for this camping class. I don't want to spend my vacation in school!

I wish I could just stay home and hang out with my two best friends, Cassie and Mandy. But everyone in my family thinks I'm crazy. They all say I'll have a great time. When you come from a big family, it's hard to argue with so many people.

There's my dad and my two older sisters, D.J. and Stephanie. But that's not all.

My mom died when I was little. So my uncle Jesse moved in to help Dad take care of us. So did Joey Gladstone. He's my dad's best friend from college. It's almost like having three dads. But that's still not all!

First Uncle Jesse got married to Becky Donaldson. Then they had twin boys, Nicky and Alex. The twins are four years old now. And they're so cute.

That's nine people. Our dog, Comet, makes ten. Sure it gets kind of crazy sometimes. But I wouldn't change it for anything. It's so much fun to live in a full house!

FULL HOUSE™ MICHELLE novels

The Great Pet Project
The Super-Duper Sleepover Party
My Two Best Friends
Lucky, Lucky Day
The Ghost in My Closet
Ballet Surprise
Major League Trouble
My Fourth-Grade Mess
Bunk 3, Teddy and Me
My Best Friend Is a Movie Star! (Super Special)
The Big Turkey Escape
The Substitute Teacher
Calling All Planets
I've Got a Secret
How to Be Cool
The Not-So-Great Outdoors

Available from MINSTREL Books

FULL HOUSE™
Michelle

The Not-So-Great Outdoors

Jean Waricha

A Parachute Press Book

Published by POCKET BOOKS
New York   London   Toronto   Sydney   Tokyo   Singapore

A MINSTREL PAPERBACK *Original*

 A Minstrel Book published by
POCKET BOOKS, a division of Simon & Schuster Inc.
1230 Avenue of the Americas, New York, NY 10020

A PARACHUTE PRESS BOOK

 READING Copyright © and ™ 1997 by Warner Bros.

FULL HOUSE, characters, names and all related indicia are trademarks of Warner Bros. © 1997.

ISBN: 0-671-00835-8

First Minstrel Books printing September 1997

10 9 8 7 6 5 4 3 2 1

A MINSTREL BOOK and colophon are registered trademarks of Simon & Schuster Inc.

Cover photo by Schultz Photography

Printed in the U.S.A.

Chapter

1

♥ "Dad, did you remember to pack marsh-mallows?" Michelle Tanner asked. Danny, Stephanie, D.J., and Michelle couldn't go on their camping trip to Yosemite National Park without marshmallows!

Camping wasn't camping without s'mores—toasted marshmallows and chocolate bars stuffed between two graham crackers. Yum, yum!

Eating s'mores was fun. But making them was even better. Michelle loved putting marshmallows on a stick and holding them over the campfire until they were a perfect golden brown.

"Dad? Marshmallows?" Michelle repeated.

Danny Tanner didn't answer. He had his nose glued to a cookbook called *10 Great Healthy Gourmet Meals for Camping Cookouts.*

Oh, no, Michelle thought. I bet there are no marshmallows in healthy gourmet meals!

She knelt down on the kitchen floor and started pawing through one of the boxes of supplies. She saw pots, pans, and a billion kinds of cleaning stuff—but no marshmallows.

Michelle shoved her strawberry-blond hair away from her face and moved on to the next box. Marshmallows, she thought. Please let there be marshmallows.

She found knives, forks, spoons, plates, cloth napkins, and a little iron. Michelle couldn't believe this.

2

Danny put down the cookbook and picked up a big pot from the counter. "Does this one look a little dirty to you?" he asked. "I bet Joey washed this one!"

"I heard that, Danny," Joey said as he hurried through the kitchen door with Jesse right behind him. "I did not wash that pot."

"I can see that," Danny answered. He turned on the water and started to scrub the pot himself.

"No, I mean *I* didn't wash that pot— Jesse did!" Joey explained.

Jesse grabbed the pot from Danny. He held it up and studied it. "This pot is super clean," he announced.

Danny never thought Joey and Jesse got things clean enough. They had both lived with the Tanners since Michelle's mother died when Michelle was a little girl. Joey was Danny's best friend from college. He had an apartment in the basement.

3

And Michelle's uncle Jesse lived upstairs with his wife, Becky, and their four-year-old twins, Nicky and Alex. Michelle loved living in such a full house.

"That pot is not—" Danny began to explain.

"Can we forget about the pot?" Michelle interrupted. "I don't see why we need all these pots and pans anyway. Or all this cleaning stuff. *Or* the iron!"

"An iron?" Joey and Jesse asked together.

"Okay, so maybe we don't need an iron. But the cleaning stuff stays," Danny said. "It can get very messy out in the wilderness," he added.

"Oh, yeah." Joey laughed. "When those marshmallows stick to you, look out!"

"Marshmallows? We're not bringing marshmallows," Danny answered.

"But, Dad," Michelle protested. "We

4

can't go camping without marshmallows to roast over the fire!"

Danny held up the *10 Great Healthy Gourmet Meals for Camping Cookouts* book. "I'm going to make you and your sisters some great gourmet dinners," Danny said. "I have all the ingredients packed."

Michelle gave a big sigh.

"Don't worry, there are some great dessert recipes in here," Danny told her. "You're going to love Yosemite, Michelle. There are all kinds of great hiking trails and things to see. Plus I have a great surprise for you."

What next? Michelle thought. Her dad just didn't understand about camping.

"You're going to love this, Michelle," Danny said. "I signed you up for a three-day camping class!"

"A what?" Jesse asked.

That's exactly what Michelle wanted to know!

"A special three-day camping class," Danny repeated. "You'll be able to learn all kinds of neat outdoor skills!"

"Just like school," Michelle muttered.

"Just like school!" Danny beamed at her. He packed his cookbook and the big pot into an empty box.

Michelle loved Mrs. Yoshida's fourth-grade class. But she didn't want to spend her camping trip in school! "Uh, Dad," she began to say.

Before Michelle could continue, D.J., Michelle's eighteen-year-old sister, and Stephanie, her thirteen-year-old sister, squeezed into the crowded kitchen.

"Do they have to take the camping class?" Michelle asked, pointing at her sisters.

"No, I think they already had enough camping experience," Danny answered.

Michelle couldn't believe it. A class that only she had to go to. Gourmet dinners. No marshmallows.

And her dad called this a camping trip? No way!

Michelle wished she could just stay home and hang out with her best friends, Cassie and Mandy, over the four-day weekend.

This was going to be the worst vacation of her life!

Chapter 2

♥ "Uh, Dad, are there supposed to be little green things in the blackberry syrup?" Michelle asked at breakfast the next morning. She gave one of her pancakes a poke.

Danny sat on a boulder across the campfire from Michelle and her sisters. They perched on a big log at one end of their campsite. Michelle noticed D.J. and Stephanie weren't eating their pancakes either.

"Those are fresh mint leaves," Michelle's dad answered. "The gourmet recipe book said they give syrup a tangy flavor. Try it."

Michelle didn't want to ask what the lumpy things in the pancakes were.

"I'm pretty full," D.J. said.

Ha! Michelle thought. D.J. had eaten only about half a bite of her breakfast.

"Me too," Stephanie added.

"Me three," Michelle chimed in quickly.

"Would you look at these sticky plates," Danny commented as he gathered up the breakfast dishes. "Good thing I brought a jumbo bottle of dishwashing soap."

"Can we go for a hike this morning?" Stephanie asked.

"Sure," Danny told her. "You and D.J. can do the dishes while I take Michelle to her camping class. Then we'll hit the trail."

"Please, Dad, can't I go with you guys instead?" Michelle begged.

Danny shook his head. "I'll feel better knowing you have some basic outdoor skills," he said. "Besides, the class is going to be fun."

Michelle started to stand up. "Hey!" she exclaimed. "I'm stuck!"

Gooey, sticky blackberry-and-mint-leaf syrup ran down the side of her shorts and formed a little puddle on the log.

"The syrup glued me here," Michelle cried. She grabbed the material of her shorts in both hands and pulled herself free.

"You're supposed to eat the syrup, Michelle, not wear it," D.J. joked.

"Purple and green are *not* your colors," Stephanie teased.

"Ha, ha. Very funny," Michelle said. "Not."

Danny ran over to Michelle's tent and ducked inside. He returned with a towel and a clean pair of shorts.

"There are some outdoor showers down that path," Danny told her. "Go wash off.

I'll try to get that blackberry stain off your shorts later. It's a good thing I brought my stain remover."

Michelle took the towel and shorts and slowly made her way to the showers. She stepped into one of the wooden shower stalls and tossed her clean shorts and her towel over the door.

"Yuck," she whispered as she stripped off her gooey shorts. She threw them and the rest of her clothes over the door too. Then she turned around and tried to figure out how to start the water.

I guess I pull this cord, she thought. Michelle tugged it—and a flood of water poured over her.

"Aaaggghhh!" she screamed. The water was icy cold.

Michelle shivered as she scrubbed off the blackberry syrup. Then she grabbed her towel and dried off as fast as she could. She couldn't wait to get dressed. She was freezing!

Michelle reached for her clean shorts—but they were gone.

All her clothes were gone!

Don't panic, she thought. They can't be gone. Maybe they just fell.

Michelle crouched down and peered under the shower door. Nothing.

"Where are my clothes?" she shrieked. No answer—except the squawk of a blue jay.

Now what was she going to do? Her dad was too far away to hear her if she yelled for help.

Michelle wrapped her big beach towel tightly around herself and tucked in the ends. She would have to make a run for it—and hope nobody saw her. That would be *sooo* embarrassing.

Michelle checked both ways to make

sure the coast was clear. Okay, she told herself. One, two, three—*go!*

She dashed out of the shower. She sped around a curve in the path—and almost ran into a girl around her age.

The girl wore a yellow T-shirt with white shorts. Her white socks had yellow trim. Her white sneakers had stars on them. And her blond hair was pulled into two pigtails—with white ribbons.

The girl's green eyes were opened wide. She stared at Michelle without blinking. "Do you always walk around in the woods in a towel?" she finally asked.

"No. Someone stole my clothes!" Michelle explained. She felt her face heat up.

"Uh, were they two pairs of shorts and a blue T-shirt?" the girl asked.

"Yeah! Did you see them? Where are they?" Michelle cried.

"I moved them to the shelf above the shower," the girl answered. "That *is* where you are supposed to put clothes. They get all wet if you hang them over the door."

"You did what?" Michelle yelled. She was out in the middle of the woods dressed in a *towel*. She was freezing. And it was all this girl's fault!

"Everyone knows that's where clothes belong. I was sure whoever was in the shower would find them," the girl replied calmly.

"That was a really stupid thing to do." Michelle glared at the girl.

"No," the girl snapped. "Hanging your clothes on the shower door was a really stupid thing to do!" The girl glared right back.

Michelle stomped past the girl. She wasn't going to waste any more time talking to her.

"Hey!" the girl called after her. "What's your name?"

Michelle turned around, but kept walking backward. "Michelle," she answered.

"I'm Elizabeth," the girl answered. "You might want to put some clothes on, Michelle. It's kind of cold out here in the woods." She grinned.

Michelle took a deep breath. Then she marched back toward the showers to get her clothes. She could hear Elizabeth giggling behind her.

I knew this camping trip was going to be bad, Michelle thought. But I didn't know it was going to be *this* bad.

I wonder what horrible thing is going to happen next?

Chapter 3

♥ "Hi, Michelle."

Oh, no, Michelle thought when she walked into her camping class an hour later. Oh, no. Oh, no! There was Elizabeth, the girl who stole her clothes. She waved to Michelle from across the room.

Michelle ignored her. She never wanted to talk to Elizabeth again. She searched the room for an empty seat. There was only one left—and it was right next to Elizabeth.

Great, just great, Michelle thought. She

crossed over to the empty seat and sat down. She was careful not to look in Elizabeth's direction. She stared around the classroom. Drawings of plants and animals covered the walls.

Michelle noticed that Elizabeth was the only kid her age. Oh, well, she thought. I can hang out by myself if I have to.

"I see you found your clothes," Elizabeth said. Her voice was loud enough for everyone in the class to hear. One of the older boys snickered.

"Yes, no thanks to you," Michelle snapped.

"Are you always this cranky?" Elizabeth asked. "Because it says in my camping manual you can make this tea out of bark that makes you super calm. I could—"

"I don't want any more help from you," Michelle answered. She kept her eyes locked on the front of the room.

"Fine," Elizabeth shot back.

"Fine," Michelle repeated.

A young woman with brown eyes and long brown hair hurried into the classroom. She wore a park ranger's uniform—knee-length green shorts and a white blouse. And she carried a large cardboard box under her arm.

"Good morning, everyone," she said in a soft voice. She put the cardboard box down on her desk. "I'm Ms. Wilson, your camping teacher. Thank you for signing up for this class."

"Thank my dad," Michelle muttered.

Elizabeth poked her in the arm. "Shhh. I'm trying to listen," she whispered.

"By the time you finish this course, you will all be expert campers." Ms. Wilson smiled at Michelle.

Michelle smiled back. Ms. Wilson seemed nice. Maybe this won't be so bad after all, she thought. As long as I can get away from Elizabeth.

"During each of our three classes I'll give you an assignment," Ms. Wilson explained. "Then I'll give you points depending on how well you do. The person with the most points at the end of the course will be named top camper. And he or she will win this."

Ms. Wilson opened the box and pulled out a wooden trophy in the shape of a chipmunk. That would look so cool on my dresser, Michelle thought.

Elizabeth poked Michelle again. "I'm going to win that trophy," she whispered.

"Forget about it. *I'm* winning the trophy," Michelle whispered back.

Ms. Wilson reached into the box again and pulled out a stack of super-thick camping manuals. When she handed Michelle hers, Michelle flipped right to the back. Two hundred pages! "I hope we don't have to read the whole thing in three days," she joked.

"Only half," Ms. Wilson joked back. She started to hand a manual to Elizabeth.

"I have my own," Elizabeth bragged. She shot a glance at Michelle. "And I've already read the whole thing. Actually, I've practically memorized it."

Ms. Wilson winked at Michelle. "Sounds like I'll have to stay on my toes! We have an expert in the class."

Elizabeth smirked. "Yep, I'm going to win that trophy for sure," she announced.

No way was Michelle going to let that annoying girl win anything.

That trophy is mine, Michelle thought. And I don't need a manual to get it!

Chapter

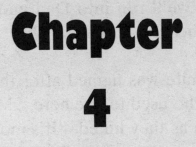

4

♥ "Okay, enough talk," Ms. Wilson said. "Let's go on a hike. It's much too beautiful here at Yosemite National Park to spend the day indoors."

Yay! Maybe this isn't going to be like school after all, Michelle thought.

Ms. Wilson led the way out of the classroom and over to one of the hiking trails. Elizabeth stuck right behind the teacher, so Michelle stayed near the back of the group.

She had had enough of Elizabeth for one day. For one life!

Maybe we'll run into Dad and D.J. and Steph, Michelle thought. That would be fun.

"Yosemite was named after the tribe of Indians who used to live here," Ms. Wilson told them as they hiked. "It's most famous for its three groves of—"

"Sequoia trees," Elizabeth interrupted.

"That's right," Ms. Wilson said.

Show-off! Michelle thought.

Ms. Wilson continued telling them about the park—with Elizabeth interrupting every few seconds.

"Let's take a breather," Ms. Wilson called when they reached a large clearing.

Michelle plopped down on the ground. She noticed Elizabeth pull out a large square of canvas from her backpack. She spread it out on the grass and then positioned herself on top of it.

Of course, Michelle thought. She wouldn't want to get her perfect white shorts dirty.

"While you rest, I'm going to rope off a section of the woods for your first assignment," Ms. Wilson told them. She pulled a long piece of rope out of her backpack. She tied one end to a big pine tree, then headed into the forest.

I wonder what she's going to have us do? Michelle thought. Whatever it was, Michelle had to earn a lot of points if she wanted to win the top-camper trophy.

About ten minutes later, Ms. Wilson re-appeared. She sat down in the middle of the group. "Okay, how many of you could find your way back to our classroom from here?"

Uh-oh, Michelle thought. Is that our first assignment? She had no idea how to get back. They had made so many twists and turns on their way here. And the park was full of trails. How would she know which one led in the right direction?

She glanced around. None of the other

kids were raising their hands. Elizabeth flipped through the pages of her camping manual with a big frown on her face.

Ms. Wilson laughed. "Don't worry," she said. "I really didn't expect any of you to know."

Michelle relaxed.

"But what you need to know," Ms. Wilson added, "is what to do if you got lost out here in the woods with no shelter."

Michelle shivered. She didn't like to think about being out in the woods all alone. She bet it could get really spooky at night.

"What would you do, Michelle?" Ms. Wilson asked.

Michelle thought for a second, but she couldn't come up with a good answer. She shrugged her shoulders. "I don't know," she admitted. "My dad always told me to call a taxi if I got lost."

Everyone laughed.

"There are no phones out here—and no taxis either," Ms. Wilson answered. She smiled at Michelle.

Elizabeth raised her hand in the air and waved it wildly. "I know, I know!"

"Yes, Elizabeth," Ms. Wilson said.

"The manual says that you should build a shelter." Elizabeth held up the thick book. "It's right here on page twenty-five."

"That's right," Ms. Wilson said.

Elizabeth turned toward Michelle. "I'm going to win," she mouthed.

"When you get lost, it's best to stay where you are—not wander around getting more lost!" Ms. Wilson continued. "And while you wait for help, you may need protection from the cold or rain or even the sun."

Ms. Wilson stood up. "Time for some hands-on experience," she told them.

"Here's your first assignment—I want each of you to build a shelter."

Elizabeth waved her hand in the air.

"Yes, Elizabeth," Ms. Wilson said.

"What are we supposed to build the shelter out of?" Elizabeth asked.

Michelle was wondering the same thing.

"There are lots of building materials out here. You just have to look hard—and use your imagination. I want you all to stay within the roped-off area. But other than that, anything goes!" Ms. Wilson answered. "Have fun!"

Michelle pushed herself to her feet. She hurried across the clearing toward the woods. That's where I'll find stuff, she thought.

She passed Elizabeth, who hadn't moved from her spot. She was busily studying her camping manual.

"I'm giving you all an hour and a half," Ms. Wilson called. "Pretend a storm is coming and you have to get your shelter up fast."

Michelle checked her bright pink watch—eleven-twenty. Okay, I have to be finished by ten to one. She set the alarm for five after twelve, so she would know when her time was halfway up.

She glanced back at Elizabeth. She was still reading the manual. "The answer has to be in here somewhere," she mumbled.

Good, Michelle thought. I hope she spends the whole hour and a half sitting there!

Michelle slowly walked into the woods. She scanned the forest floor, searching for . . . anything. Anything she could use to make a shelter.

Pinecones? Could she make a shelter with pinecones?

No. It would be too hard to stick them together.

What else. Rocks? Michelle had seen

walls made of rocks stacked on top of each other.

No. It would take forever to gather enough rocks to make a shelter. Besides, the really good ones would be too heavy to carry.

Tree branches? Yes! Tree branches would make a great shelter, Michelle thought. She gathered as many branches as she could carry and hauled them back to the clearing.

"What are you doing with all those branches?" Elizabeth demanded. She sat in the same spot in the clearing.

Michelle didn't answer. She wasn't going to give Elizabeth any help.

"You aren't planning to use them to build your shelter, are you?" Elizabeth asked. She got up and hurried over to Michelle. "Because that's a really silly idea. I just found the section on shelters in the manual. Do you want to know what it says?"

"No," Michelle answered.

Elizabeth began to read again. "Oh, no," she whispered. "This can't be right."

"What?" Michelle asked.

Elizabeth ignored her. She darted off into the woods without another word.

What a weird girl, Michelle thought.

Michelle glanced down at her pile of branches. I need more, she decided. A lot more. She made three more trips into the woods. By the time she had gathered enough branches, blisters were forming on her hands and sweat was trickling down her forehead.

Michelle knelt on the ground and dug a small, deep hole. Then she took one of her branches and stuck it in the hole. She refilled the hole with dirt, packing it tightly around the branch.

When she was finished, the branch stuck straight up—all by itself. Perfect.

Michelle kept working until she had four low walls made of branches. Okay, now I need a roof, she thought. She grabbed one of the longest branches left in her pile. She stood on tiptoe and draped the branch over two of the walls.

This is going to work! As fast as she could, Michelle added branches to her roof. When she had used every branch in her pile, she stepped back and studied her shelter.

I did it! Yay! she thought.

Elizabeth hurried past her, heading for the woods. "What if it rains?" she called. "The *manual* says you need to protect yourself in case of rain. And the rain will go right through those branches. You'll get all soaked."

"I don't care what the manual says!" Michelle yelled.

"Okay," Elizabeth shouted over her shoulder. "But don't come crying to me when it rains and you get all wet."

Michelle stared at her shelter. She's right, Michelle thought. Elizabeth is right. Rain would go right through Michelle's roof.

I need something to cover the roof, she thought. But what?

Michelle headed back into the woods. Thinking, thinking, thinking. She kicked her way through the leaves on the ground.

Then she stopped and snapped her fingers. Leaves! That's it. She would spread leaves on top of the branches. That would keep out the rain!

Michelle gathered a huge armful of leaves and rushed back to the clearing. She didn't have much time to spare!

Elizabeth passed Michelle with more branches. "You know," she began. "The *manual* says—"

"Stop!" Michelle cried. "I told you I don't care what the manual says. I don't want any help from you!"

Elizabeth backed up a step. "You don't want my advice?"

"No! Not now, not ever!" Michelle yelled.

"Fine!" Elizabeth snapped. "Then I guess you don't want to know that those leaves are poison ivy!"

Chapter

5

♥ Poison ivy!

Michelle's whole body started to itch. Her arms. Her legs. Even her ears!

She jumped around, trying to scratch everywhere at once.

Everyone in the class turned and looked at her. And Elizabeth started to laugh.

"What's so funny?" Michelle shouted.

Elizabeth's face turned red. She was laughing so hard, she could hardly talk. "That's not poison ivy! I was just joking!"

Michelle stopped scratching.

Elizabeth pulled in a big gulp of air. "But how would you know that?" she asked. "Since you refuse to look at the *manual?*"

Michelle lunged at Elizabeth. She wanted to grab her stupid manual and tear it into a billion pieces.

"What's wrong, girls?" Ms. Wilson called. She hurried over to them.

Michelle froze. "Nothing, Ms. Wilson," she answered. "I thought I touched poison ivy. But I guess I didn't."

Ms. Wilson studied Michelle's pile of leaves. "Nope," she agreed. "No poison ivy there."

She walked around Michelle's shelter, examining it carefully. "Did you build this, Michelle?" she asked.

"Yes," Michelle answered.

"This is very good," Ms. Wilson said. "What are the leaves for?"

"I was going to cover my roof with

them. That way I would stay dry if it rained," Michelle explained.

Ms. Wilson nodded. "That's a great idea. Leaves make very good cover."

Michelle gave Elizabeth a triumphant smile. Elizabeth stuck her chin in the air and ignored her.

"Everyone! Over here!" Ms. Wilson called. The other students gathered around her.

"See, class," Mrs. Wilson said. "I told you there were a lot of things in the woods that would make a good shelter. You just have to use your imagination—like Michelle did."

Ms. Wilson patted Michelle on the shoulder. "Good work, Michelle. You get full points for this assignment."

"Come look at my shelter, Ms. Wilson," one of the boys called.

Mrs. Wilson followed the boy across the

clearing. Michelle started after them—and gasped.

A shelter almost identical to hers stood halfway across the clearing. Michelle hurried over to it.

"That's mine," Elizabeth bragged. Michelle spun around and found Elizabeth right behind her.

"You said using branches was silly!" Michelle cried. "You just wanted to use them yourself. What a cheater!"

"I did think it was silly. Then I found the section on shelters in the manual—and it said to use branches. So I did!" Elizabeth shot back.

Michelle ran her hand over the side of Elizabeth's shelter. "You even dug holes the same way I did!" she accused.

Elizabeth's shelter swayed back and forth. Back and forth.

"What did you do?" Elizabeth cried.

Crash! The shelter collapsed. The branches fell into a huge pile.

They look like pick-up sticks, Michelle thought.

"You wrecked my shelter!" Elizabeth yelled.

"I did not! I barely touched it!" Michelle yelled back.

"It wouldn't have fallen down if you *barely* touched it!" Elizabeth shouted.

Ms. Wilson ran up beside them. "Now what, girls?" she asked.

"Michelle knocked over my shelter," Elizabeth accused.

"I did not. It fell over." Michelle stared up at Ms. Wilson. "Really."

Ms. Wilson bent down and studied what was left of Elizabeth's project. "I think I see the problem," she said. "You just didn't dig the holes deep enough, Elizabeth. But it was a good try." She left to finish judging the rest of the class's shelters.

Elizabeth glared at Michelle. "I followed the instructions in the manual exactly," she said. "I know my shelter wouldn't have collapsed if you hadn't shoved it."

"No way! You heard what Ms. Wilson said," Michelle protested.

"You were still mad at me for fooling you about the poison ivy. And moving your clothes this morning. You wrecked my project just to get back at me," Elizabeth said.

Michelle turned around and walked away. Nothing she could say would convince Elizabeth that she didn't try to destroy her shelter.

Why even bother? Michelle thought. I never want to talk to her again anyway.

*   *   *

"How was your first outdoor skills class?" Danny asked.

Michelle dragged herself over to the fallen log and flopped down on it. "It was good. We built shelters—and I got more points than anyone for mine. But I'm so tired," Michelle answered.

"Not too tired for a surprise, I hope," her dad said. "I met some other campers this morning—and one of them loaned me some bleach."

"Bleach? That's the big surprise?"

"Well, I needed some to get that blackberry juice out of your shorts," Danny said. "I can't believe I forgot to pack any."

"Uh, thanks," Michelle said.

Danny laughed. "Don't worry. That's not the surprise. The woman who gave me the bleach has a daughter around your age. I thought you would want to meet her, so I invited the whole family for dinner."

Cool! Michelle thought. After a day spent with Elizabeth, Michelle was ready to make a new friend.

"Hey, here they are!" Danny stood up and waved.

Michelle turned around—and her stomach twisted into a zillion little knots.

Elizabeth was walking straight toward her with a huge grin on her face!

Chapter 6

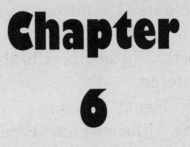

 "You could learn a lot about camping from Elizabeth," Danny said at breakfast the next morning. "The facts she read from that manual were fascinating."

"Yeah, I could have listened to Elizabeth all night," Stephanie agreed. "Can you believe Yosemite Falls is twice as tall as the Empire State Building? That's amazing."

"And remember what Elizabeth told us about birds?" D.J. asked. "She said there were more than two hundred species in the park. I want to see how many I can spot."

"Elizabeth, Elizabeth, Elizabeth," Michelle muttered.

"What?" Danny asked.

"Nothing," Michelle answered. She took a big bite of her dad's special Spanish omelette.

Her whole family *loooved* Elizabeth. It made Michelle sick.

Why couldn't they see what a know-it-all Elizabeth was? Why couldn't they see that all she cared about was making Michelle look dumb?

"Time for your class, Michelle," Danny said.

Michelle handed him her breakfast plate. "Thanks for not putting any weird stuff in the omelette, Dad," she said.

"I'm glad you don't think day lily tubers are weird," he answered.

"What?" D.J. exclaimed.

"What are tubers?" Stephanie demanded.

"They're roots," Danny said. "They're good for you."

"Yuck!" Michelle said. "We ate roots."

"Come on. Where's your spirit of adventure?" he asked. "Besides, it's no different from eating a potato."

The beeper on Michelle's watch went off. "Got to go," she told them.

"See you later, Tanner-gator," Steph said.

"Bye!" Michelle started down the path toward the classroom.

"Say hi to Elizabeth for us," Danny called after her.

Yeah, right, Michelle thought. I'm not even going to say hi to Elizabeth for *myself.*

Michelle picked up her pace. She couldn't wait to get to class. She wondered what today's assignment would be.

Whatever it is, I'm going to beat Elizabeth, Michelle promised herself.

When I win that top-camper trophy, it will show Dad that Elizabeth can learn something from *me!* And Elizabeth will have to admit that she doesn't know more about camping than everyone in the whole wide world!

Michelle practically skipped into class.

"You look happy this morning, Michelle," Ms. Wilson commented.

"I am," she answered. Because today I'm going to get one step closer to winning my trophy, she thought.

Michelle took her seat next to Elizabeth. It was the only one empty again.

"Your family is really nice," Elizabeth whispered. "Where did they find you?"

Michelle kept her eyes focused on the trophy on Ms. Wilson's desk. Elizabeth won't be making jokes when I win that trophy, she thought.

"Okay, everyone," Ms. Wilson called. "How many different kinds of animals do you think we have here in Yosemite National Park."

Elizabeth's hand shot up.

"Sam, what do you think?" Ms. Wilson asked.

"Uh, about twenty-five?" a blond boy about Stephanie's age answered.

"More than that. How about you, Michelle?" Ms. Wilson said.

Elizabeth said there were more than two hundred kinds of birds. So there were probably at least that many animals, Michelle decided. "Two hundred and fifty," she declared.

Elizabeth snickered.

"Not quite that many."

Elizabeth wiggled her fingers. She waved her hand as hard as she could.

"Elizabeth?" Ms. Wilson said.

"Exactly sixty-three, according to page

thirty-five of the manual," Elizabeth announced.

"That's correct—more or less. Some of the critters don't like to be counted, so we may have missed a few!" Ms. Wilson said. "Today we're going to see how many of those animals we can spot. We're going on another hike. But we need to move slowly and quietly, so we don't scare any of the animals away."

"Do you think we'll see any bears?" someone asked as they trooped out of the classroom.

"Probably not," Ms. Wilson said. "We do have bears at Yosemite, but they don't usually get too close to campers."

Whew! Michelle thought. That's good news.

Michelle heard Elizabeth give a sigh of relief behind her.

Ms. Wilson led them out of the classroom down a path to a waterfall. "This is called Bridalveil Fall," she told them. "Let's stand there for a minute and see what we can see."

"There's a squirrel," someone whispered.

"And a chipmunk," another kid added.

Something brushed against Michelle's foot. She jumped.

"What is it, Michelle?" Ms. Wilson asked.

"I don't know," Michelle answered. "I just felt something move by my foot."

"Maybe it's a snake!" Elizabeth cried.

"Shhh. Everybody hold still. If it's a snake, we don't want to scare it away."

"We don't?" Michelle whispered.

Ms. Wilson slowly made her way over to Michelle. She knelt down next to her and studied the grass at the edge of the path. "There he is!"

She motioned everyone closer and pointed to a spot a few feet away from Michelle. "See?"

Michelle gave a little gasp when she spotted the brown snake. It was longer than her arm.

Ms. Wilson slowly stretched her hand toward the snake. Then with one quick movement, she grabbed it behind its head. Its tail whipped back and forth until she caught it with her other hand.

"A lot of people think snakes are slimy. But they are actually dry and pleasant to the touch." Ms. Wilson smiled at them. "I just decided what your assignment for the day will be."

I don't want to hear this, Michelle thought.

"Each of you who takes a turn holding this gopher snake will earn full points for the day," Ms. Wilson continued.

I knew I didn't want to hear it.

"Is it poisonous?" someone called.

"Of course not," Ms. Wilson answered. "I wouldn't ask you to do anything that could hurt you. But even though the snake isn't poisonous, he can bite. That's why you have to hold him behind his head the way I am right now. In this position, he can't reach you to bite you."

Michelle caught a glimpse of the snake's white fangs. She shivered. She wasn't sure she could do this. Trophy or no trophy.

"You aren't afraid of a little snake, are you?" Elizabeth whispered in her ear.

"No way," Michelle answered.

"Okay, who wants to go first?" Ms. Wilson asked.

Elizabeth's hand shot up faster than anyone else's. Of course.

Ms. Wilson gently transferred the snake into Elizabeth's hands. "It's really smooth," Elizabeth said. She didn't sound one bit nervous.

Elizabeth handed the snake to a boy in back of Michelle.

It will be my turn soon, Michelle

thought. She took a deep, shaky breath. If Elizabeth can do it, I can do it, she told herself.

Michelle felt something cold on the back of her neck.

Cold and slimy.

"The snake!" she screamed.

Michelle tried to slap it away. But it slithered underneath her T-shirt and down her bare back.

Chapter 7

♥ "Get it off me!" Michelle shrieked. "The snake is sliding down my back! Get it off me!"

"Michelle, calm down," Ms. Wilson said firmly. "I have the snake right here. Look, Michelle. I have the snake right here."

Michelle forced her gaze over to Ms. Wilson's hands. She *was* holding the gopher snake.

"But something's on my back!" Michelle cried. "I can feel it."

Ms. Wilson gave the snake to Elizabeth.

She hurried behind Michelle and ran her hands over Michelle's back.

"Got it," Ms. Wilson said. "It's just a little earthworm. Nothing to be scared of. Are you okay?"

Michelle nodded. "That was gross!" she exclaimed.

Everyone in the class laughed. Elizabeth laughed the loudest.

"That's enough," Ms. Wilson called. "Now, who wants the next turn holding the snake?"

Sam raised his hand, and Elizabeth handed over the snake. After each kid had a turn, Ms. Wilson turned to Michelle. "Are you ready to hold him?" she asked.

"Yes," Michelle answered. She reached out her hands and squeezed her eyes shut. She couldn't stand to watch.

"You have to open your eyes," Ms. Wilson said. "You'll drop him if you don't."

Michelle slowly obeyed. But she couldn't

stop her hands from shaking. She couldn't stop thinking about that snake wriggling down her back.

Even though it turned out not to be a snake.

"He's more afraid of you than you are of him, I bet," Ms. Wilson coaxed.

"I can't!" Michelle exclaimed.

"That's okay. Don't worry about it. You got to see a snake up close. That's something," Ms. Wilson said. She gently replaced the snake on the ground.

"That's *nothing,*" Elizabeth said softly so no one but Michelle could hear.

Wait, Michelle thought. That worm couldn't have gotten on my neck by itself. Someone had to put it there.

And she knew who—Elizabeth.

"It was you! You stuck that worm on me!" she cried.

"So now we're even," Elizabeth snapped. "You messed up my shelter, and I messed up your wildlife test. Now we can have a fair competition!"

"This means war!" Michelle declared.

"Isn't the lake beautiful?" Ms. Wilson asked the class the next day. She had spent the morning teaching them how to paddle a canoe safely. Now it was time for their assignment—paddling across the lake and back.

"For our last class I want you to work in pairs," Ms. Wilson continued. "It's best to start out with two people about the same size. Michelle and Elizabeth—why don't you two work together?"

Michelle and Elizabeth stared at each other as Ms. Wilson broke the rest of the class into pairs.

I'd rather be partners with a skunk, Michelle though.

"I hope you were listening when Ms.

Wilson was teaching us how to paddle," Elizabeth said.

"Of course I was listening," Michelle answered. She marched over to an empty canoe, Elizabeth right behind her. Michelle grabbed the front of the canoe. Elizabeth grabbed the back. They hauled it down to the lake.

Michelle grabbed a life jacket and strapped it on. So did Elizabeth. They climbed into the canoe without a word.

Michelle clenched her paddle in both hands. She pulled it through the water as hard as she could. She'd show Elizabeth who knew how to canoe!

Michelle paddled until her arms ached— but they weren't even halfway across the lake.

"You're paddling all wrong!" Elizabeth yelled. "Let me show you in the manual."

"I am not!" Michelle shouted back. She didn't stop paddling.

"We're going in circles!" Elizabeth cried.

"Then you must be the one who's paddling wrong!" Michelle shot back.

Michelle whipped around to face Elizabeth—and almost whacked her in the head with her paddle.

Elizabeth jerked back—and her paddle flew out of her hands. It landed in the lake with a splash!

"Now look what you made me do," Elizabeth complained. She leaned over and tried to grab her paddle. But she couldn't quite reach it.

"I'll get it," Michelle told her. "Just calm down." Michelle leaned over too.

And the canoe began to tip.

Michelle threw herself toward the other side of the canoe. But it was too late.

Ker-plunk!

Michelle fell into the lake.

Ker-plunk!

Elizabeth landed in the lake too.

Ice-cold water shot up Michelle's nose. She started to choke.

She spit out a mouthful of water and drew in a long breath. At least I have my life jacket on, she thought. She began to swim toward shore. Elizabeth swam right behind her.

When they reached the shallow part of the lake, they scrambled to their feet. They began to wade. Michelle struggled to move her legs through the cold, cold water.

"I can't believe you did that!" Elizabeth exploded. "Nice going!"

"Me? It was your fault!" Michelle insisted.

"Look at me. My hair is soaking wet. My clothes are ruined. And it *was* your fault. If you had bothered to read the manual—"

Elizabeth stopped. She stood in the lake with a horrified expression on her face.

"My manual!" She turned back toward the overturned canoe. "Where is my manual?"

"Forget your stupid manual!" Michelle said. "It has to be completely soaked."

"Michelle Tanner and Elizabeth Brown—get out of the water right now!" Ms. Wilson yelled.

She sounds really mad, Michelle thought. Michelle trudged out of the water with Elizabeth on her heels.

Ms. Wilson handed Michelle and Elizabeth towels when they reached the shore. "I'm very disappointed in both of you," she said sternly. "Did either of you listen to my talk on water safety?"

"Yes," Michelle answered.

"Yes," Elizabeth repeated.

"Well, I couldn't tell by watching you two. Michelle, you could have knocked Elizabeth unconscious with your paddle. And you both helped tip that canoe over."

Ms. Wilson shook her head. "I'm afraid

I'm going to have to eliminate both of you from the top-camper competition."

"Can't we have another chance?" Elizabeth begged.

"Please," Michelle added.

"I'm sorry, girls. But after what happened today, I can't even consider awarding the trophy to either of you."

Chapter

8

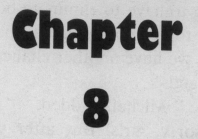 "What happened to you?" Danny exclaimed.

"You're all wet!" Stephanie cried.

Michelle trudged up to their campsite. Her toes squished in her waterlogged sneakers. "I fell in the lake."

"You must feel like an icicle," D.J. said. "The lake water is freezing. I didn't even want to get my feet wet when Steph and I went fishing yesterday."

"Go change your clothes before you catch cold," her father said.

Michelle hurried into her tent and changed into jeans and a sweatshirt. She didn't have another pair of shoes, so she put on her thickest pair of socks.

"We were just about to take a hike up to Tuolumne Meadows," Danny said. "We can drop you off at your class on our way."

"Can't I go with you instead? Please," Michelle begged.

"I thought you loved your class," D.J. said.

"Yeah, aren't you trying to win a trophy or something?" Stephanie asked.

Michelle stared down at her sneakers. "Um . . . not anymore," she admitted.

"Why not?" Danny said. "What's going on, Michelle?"

"It's all Elizabeth's fault!" Michelle burst out. "She made our canoe tip over. And she put a snake down my back. And she hid my clothes when I was in the shower. She's ruining the camping trip. Now I don't even have a chance at winning the trophy, and—"

"Wait, wait," Danny said. "Slow down. Elizabeth put a snake down your back?"

"Well, it was a worm, really," Michelle said. She pushed her wet hair out of her face.

"Big difference, Michelle," Stephanie said.

Michelle glared at her sister. "She wanted me to think it was a snake," Michelle answered. "That's just as bad."

"What happened in the canoe?" Danny asked.

"Elizabeth dropped her paddle. We both leaned over to get it—and we tipped over," Michelle explained.

"So it was an accident, right?"

"I guess," Michelle said. "But it wouldn't have happened if Elizabeth hadn't kept yelling at me. She said I was paddling wrong! But she was the one who was messing up."

Michelle took a deep breath. She knew she had to tell her dad the whole story. She didn't want him to hear it from Ms. Wilson—or Elizabeth!

"Then I turned around to tell her to leave me alone—and I almost hit her with the paddle. I didn't mean to, though! That's when she dropped her paddle in the lake," Michelle told Danny.

She took another deep breath and continued. "Ms. Wilson told us we were both out of the top-camper competition. And it's so unfair. We wouldn't have tipped over if Elizabeth hadn't kept shouting at me."

"It sounds as if you were both to blame," Danny said. "You have to learn to cooperate, Michelle."

"Dad speech number one hundred and three," D.J. called out. "Cooperation."

"Come on, D.J." Stephanie said. She pulled D.J. to her feet. "Let's wait in my tent. We don't need to hear this talk again!" Stephanie smiled sympathetically at Michelle as she and D.J. hurried off.

Danny shook his head. "I talk about it so much because it's important," he said. "All through your life you're going to have to be able to work with other people, Michelle. At school, when you get a job, even in your family."

"I guess," Michelle said. "But Elizabeth made me so mad."

"That's no excuse," Danny told her. "You and Elizabeth could have been seriously hurt today. You need to learn to work with other people—even if you don't like them."

"I'll try," Michelle answered.

"Good." Danny said. He glanced at his watch. "Your class is almost over, so let's all go hiking together."

Yes! Michelle thought. Today was the last class. I'm going home tomorrow. I'm never going to see Elizabeth again.

"You can make up with Elizabeth tonight," her dad told her. "We're all having dinner with Elizabeth and her parents."

"Dad, why?" Michelle moaned. "It's our last night here. Do we really have to spend it with Elizabeth?"

"I already accepted her parents' invitation," Danny said. "Besides, I think it will be good for you and Elizabeth to make up."

Make up with Miss Know-It-All? Michelle thought. Yuck!

Chapter 9

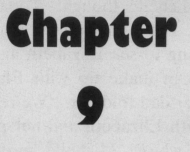

 "Hi, Elizabeth," Michelle muttered. She sat down on one of the big rocks around the Browns' campfire. She chose a rock as far away from Elizabeth as possible.

Elizabeth didn't answer. She looked mad.

What does *she* have to be mad about? Michelle thought. *I'm* the one who should be mad.

"I think we need some more wood for the fire before I cook our burgers," Mr. Brown said.

Elizabeth jumped up. "I'll go gather some!"

I bet she just wants to get away from me, Michelle thought. Fine. I like it that way.

"I'll help," Stephanie volunteered.

Elizabeth gave her a big smile. "Thanks," she said.

"Michelle, why don't you help Elizabeth," Danny said.

Michelle knew there was no way she could say no. "Okay," she answered.

Elizabeth turned around and stalked away from the campsite. Michelle trotted after her.

"Don't go too far," Mrs. Brown yelled after them. "It will be dark soon."

Elizabeth stomped into the woods.

"Slow down," Michelle complained. "There are branches all over the place we can use for the fire."

Elizabeth picked up her pace.

"I said slow down," Michelle called as she hurried to catch up. "What is your problem?"

Elizabeth spun around. "My *problem* is that because of you I'm not going to win that top-camper trophy. And it's not fair. I had the whole manual almost memorized."

"So what?" Michelle shot back. "That doesn't mean you were going to win. I had as many points as you did. If you hadn't tipped over the canoe—"

"Shhh!" Elizabeth hissed. "I heard something."

Crunch! Crunch! Crunch!

Michelle froze. Something was moving toward them.

"What is it?" Elizabeth whispered.

Crunch! Crunch! Crunch!

"I don't know," Michelle answered. "Maybe it's one of the rangers, or another camper."

"Hello," Elizabeth called. "Who's there?"

No one answered.

Crunch! Crunch! Crunch!

No one answered. The low branches on a tree near Michelle began to shake. Michelle's heart beat faster. She inched closer to Elizabeth.

"Look!" Elizabeth cried. "It's a little bear cub."

"It's so cute," Michelle said. Her heart started to slow back down. "It's like a little teddy bear."

"Yeah. I have a stuffed bear at home that looks almost like him," Elizabeth agreed.

The bear cub dropped to the ground and over onto its back. It rolled around, giving little grunts of pleasure.

Michelle giggled.

"Aw, it's so cute," Elizabeth crooned.

Grarrrh!

The loud growl sent a shiver racing

through Michelle. "That must be the cub's mother!" she exclaimed.

Michelle and Elizabeth stared at each other. "Run!" Elizabeth yelled. She took off through the forest.

Michelle took off right behind her. A branch slapped Michelle across the face, but she didn't stop. She ran and ran and ran.

She ran until her lungs burned and her legs ached. And she kept running.

Finally she had to stop. She couldn't take one more step.

Michelle bent over and braced her hands on her knees. She concentrated on pulling in deep breaths of the cool evening air. She could hear Elizabeth panting beside her.

"I think we're safe," Elizabeth said.

Michelle straightened up and looked around. The woods were still and quiet.

How long had they been running? How

far away were they from the Browns' campsite?

"Ummm . . . do you know where we are?" Michelle asked.

"I think . . ." Elizabeth studied the woods around them. "We're . . . lost!"

Chapter 10

♥ "Lost! I was following you!" Michelle shouted.

"We were getting chased by a bear!" Elizabeth yelled back. "I wasn't thinking about where I was going."

"This is just great," Michelle said. "Now what are we supposed to do?"

"Well, Ms. Wilson said to stay put when you get lost," Elizabeth said. "But it's still light. I bet I can find the way back. Follow me."

"No way," Michelle answered. "This

time you follow me! I think that tree looks familiar." She pointed to a pine tree with a big, lumpy knot on one side. "Let's go that way."

"Are you sure?" Elizabeth asked. She sounded worried.

Michelle studied the tree. "Yes," she said. She was sure she remembered the funny knot on that tree. At least she was pretty sure . . .

"Come on." Michelle led the way through the forest. She kept searching for something else that looked familiar. But she didn't see anything.

When she heard the rush of a waterfall, Michelle smiled. She knew there was a waterfall near their campsite.

Michelle loved the feel of the damp air near the waterfall. It cooled off her hot face and made her feel more energetic. "Let's hurry," she called to Elizabeth. "Our parents are probably going nuts."

They hurried through the woods. Every second Michelle expected to see a campsite.

But all she saw was more woods.

"I have to rest," Elizabeth said. "I'm pooped." She sat down under a big oak tree.

Michelle sat down next to her. She rested her head against the tree trunk and closed her eyes. She needed to think.

We should have reached the campsite by now, Michelle realized. She felt her stomach tighten. It takes only about five minutes to walk from my tent to the waterfall. What went wrong?

"Oh, no!" Elizabeth cried.

Michelle's eyes snapped open. "What?" she demanded.

Elizabeth pointed to a pine tree several feet away. "Look familiar?" she asked.

Michelle gasped. The pine tree had a big, lumpy knothole.

They were right back where they started from!

"We've been going in circles," Elizabeth declared. "And now it's getting dark."

Michelle jerked her gaze up to the sky. Elizabeth was right. The sun was almost down. And it was starting to get cold.

"But we have to be pretty near my campsite. I know the waterfall is really close to it," Michelle said.

Elizabeth snorted. "Michelle, there are tons of waterfalls in the park."

"Oh," Michelle said.

"This is your fault," Elizabeth said. "You said you knew where you were going."

"You're the one who ran all the way out here," Michelle said.

"You didn't have to follow me!" Elizabeth told her.

"I shouldn't have," Michelle answered.

"Well, don't follow me this time," Elizabeth said. "I'm going to find my own way back."

"Fine."

Michelle watched Elizabeth march off. She wrapped her arms around herself. It really is getting cold, she thought. What am I going to do?

"Elizabeth, come back!" Michelle shouted.

No answer. Elizabeth had disappeared into the woods.

Okay, Michelle told herself. I can't just take off like I did last time. I have to think.

She stared up at the sky, watching the stars come out. What should I do? she thought. But she just didn't know.

"Helllp!" someone screamed.

Michelle bolted to her feet. That's Elizabeth!

"Helllpp meeee!"

Chapter

11

♥ "I'm coming, Elizabeth!" Michelle shouted. "Keep yelling so I can find you."

"Help! Help! Help!" Elizabeth screeched.

Michelle followed the sound of Elizabeth's voice. At least there's a full moon, she thought. I would hate to walk through these woods in the pitch dark. I'd keep smacking into trees.

"I see you," Elizabeth called. She sounded relieved. "Be careful, Michelle. I fell into a gully. If you fall in too, we're really stuck."

Michelle carefully made her way to the gully. She knelt down at the edge. "Can't you climb out?" she asked Elizabeth.

"I tried," Elizabeth answered. "But the dirt keeps crumbling out from under my hands. There's nothing I can get a grip on."

Michelle thought for a moment. "I have an idea. I'll be right back."

She searched through the woods until she found a long, thick branch. Then she hauled it back over to the gully. "Move out of the way, Elizabeth," Michelle called. "I'm going to shove this branch down there."

Michelle pushed the long branch over the edge of the gully. She gripped the top tightly with both hands. "Okay, now you grab onto the bottom of the branch. I'll pull—and you can kind of walk up the wall."

Elizabeth followed Michelle's instructions. "Ready!"

Michelle leaned back and pulled on the branch with all her strength. The rough bark bit into her palms, but she didn't let go. "Come on, Elizabeth. You can do it!" she called.

Elizabeth slowly began to climb the side of the gully.

"You're doing great!" Michelle yelled. She felt the branch begin to slip through her hands. She dug her fingernails into the wood and hung on.

Elizabeth pulled herself over the edge of the gully and shoved herself to her feet.

Michelle let go of the branch and it fell to the bottom of the gully with a crash.

"You saved my life," Elizabeth said.

It felt weird to hear Elizabeth say that. Elizabeth—Miss Know-It-All. Her worst enemy.

"That's okay," Michelle mumbled. "We still have to find our way back."

"This time let's do it together," Elizabeth said. "Friends?" She stuck out her hand.

"Friends." Michelle shook Elizabeth's hand.

"Let's stay right here until we have a plan," Elizabeth suggested.

"I remember my dad telling me that our campsite was north of that sign shaped like a big bear. I saw it when we first drove in," Michelle said. "Maybe if I climb a tree, I could spot it."

"Great idea," Elizabeth said. "There's a tree with some low branches. If I gave you a boost, you could probably make it to the lowest one."

They hurried over to the tree. Elizabeth crouched down and linked her hands together. Michelle stepped up onto Elizabeth's hands, and Elizabeth boosted her high enough so she could reach the bottom branch.

Michelle swung herself onto the lowest branch, then struggled to her feet. Then she started to climb. She carefully tested each branch before she put her weight on it.

The last thing she needed was to go crashing down! The only thing worse than being lost in the woods was being lost in the woods with a broken leg.

Michelle climbed up two more branches. Then she stopped and stared around.

"I see it!" Michelle cried. "It's that way!"

Elizabeth drew an arrow in the dirt showing which direction the sign was in. "Got it," she called.

Michelle climbed to the bottom branch. She grabbed it with both hands and swung down. Then she jumped to the ground.

"Oh, no," she said. "Now we know where the sign is—but which way is north?"

"All we have to do is find the North Star. That's what it says in the manual." Elizabeth grinned at Michelle. Then she tilted back her head and studied the stars. "There it is!" She pointed the star out to Michelle.

"What are we waiting for? Let's go!" Michelle exclaimed. They hurried off toward the campsite. Then Michelle stopped dead.

"What?" Elizabeth asked.

"Just in case." Michelle took off her beaded necklace. She broke the string and let the beads run into her hand.

"I don't get it," Elizabeth said.

Michelle dropped one of the beads on the ground. "I'm going to mark our steps with the beads. That way we won't go around in a circle again."

"Good thinking," Elizabeth said. "Where did you learn that?"

"The manual," Michelle answered.

Elizabeth stared at her.

"Well, maybe it was *Hansel and Gretel,*" she admitted. "Let's get home. I'm starving."

"Me too," Elizabeth said as they headed off. "I'm going to have Dad make me three hamburgers."

"I'm glad your dad is cooking tonight," Michelle confessed. "My dad found this book of gourmet camping recipes—and they are gross!"

They walked along in silence. The only sound was their growling stomachs.

"Owww!" Elizabeth exclaimed. "A mosquito just bit me."

Michelle felt something prick her arm. "Me too."

"I just got another bite," Elizabeth complained.

Michelle got three bites at once. "They're everywhere!"

Dozens of mosquitoes buzzed and swarmed around them.

"Quick, get some mud!" Elizabeth shouted.

"Mud?" Michelle asked.

"According to the manual, mud protects people from mosquito bites," Elizabeth told her. Elizabeth found a muddy spot and smeared some mud on her legs.

"Wait," Michelle said. "I've got a better way to put on the mud.'"

"You do? How?" Elizabeth asked.

Splat! A handful of mud hit Elizabeth in the shoulder.

"Mud-ball fight!" Michelle cried.

"This means war!" Elizabeth yelled. She grabbed a clump of mud and threw it at Michelle's legs. *Splat!*

Splat! Splat! Splat!

The mud balls flew until Michelle and

Elizabeth were almost completely covered—from sneakers to ponytails.

"I give up!" Elizabeth cried. She held both hands over her head.

"No way!" Michelle called back. "This isn't over." She bent down and scooped up a double handful of mud. Then she hurled it at Elizabeth.

Elizabeth ducked—just as a man appeared from behind a tree right in back of her.

"Look out!" Michelle yelled.

Too late.

Splat! The mud ball hit the man in the face.

Uh-oh!

Michelle squinted at the man.

"Dad?"

Chapter
12

♥ "What's going on?" Michelle's dad demanded.

Mr. and Mrs. Brown, D.J., and Stephanie rushed up behind him. "We've been crazy with worry—and you two are out here playing," Danny continued.

"Elizabeth, what happened?" Mrs. Brown cried.

"It's not how it looks, Dad," Michelle said.

"She's right, Mr. Tanner," Elizabeth chimed in.

"Please explain," Mr. Brown said.

"We were about to collect some wood, and we saw a bear cub," Michelle began.

"Then we heard its mother growl," Elizabeth continued.

"So we ran," Michelle said.

"And we got lost," they said together.

"And then I fell in a gully—and Michelle had to rescue me," Elizabeth said.

Everyone stared at Michelle. "Wow," D.J. said. "You guys had an adventure."

"After that we still had to figure out how to get home. I climbed a tree and looked for that bear sign. I remembered you said our campsite was north of that, Dad," Michelle explained. "And Elizabeth knew how to tell which way north was by finding the North Star."

"That's impressive," Mrs. Brown said.

"You almost made it back," Mr. Brown told them. "We're less than half a mile from our campsite."

Danny put one arm around Michelle and the other around Elizabeth. "If you ask me, I think you both deserve the top-camper award. I'm very proud of you."

"Ouch!" Stephanie slapped her arm. "I just got bitten by a mosquito."

"I'm being eaten alive," Mrs. Brown exclaimed.

Michelle grinned at Elizabeth. Elizabeth grinned at Michelle.

"We top campers know how to deal with mosquitoes, right, Elizabeth?" Michelle asked.

"Right!" Elizabeth answered. "One, two, three . . ."

Splat!

It doesn't matter if you live around the corner...
or around the world...
If you are a fan of Mary-Kate and Ashley Olsen,
you should be a member of

MARY-KATE + ASHLEY'S FUN CLUB™

Here's what you get:
Our Funzine™
An autographed color photo
Two black & white individual photos
A full size color poster
An official **Fun Club**™ membership card
A **Fun Club**™ school folder
Two special **Fun Club**™ surprises
A holiday card
Fun Club™ collectibles catalog
Plus a **Fun Club**™ box to keep everything in

To join Mary-Kate + Ashley's Fun Club™, fill out the form
below and send it along with

U.S. Residents – $17.00
Canadian Residents – $22 U.S. Funds
International Residents – $27 U.S. Funds

MARY-KATE + ASHLEY'S FUN CLUB™
859 HOLLYWOOD WAY, SUITE 275
BURBANK, CA 91505

NAME:_____

ADDRESS:_____

_CITY:_____ STATE:_____ ZIP:_____

PHONE:(____) _____ BIRTHDATE:_____

TM & © 1996 Dualstar Entertainment Group, Inc.   1242

ᖴULL HOUSᴇ™
Stephanie

PHONE CALL FROM A FLAMINGO	88004-7/$3.99
THE BOY-OH-BOY NEXT DOOR	88121-3/$3.99
TWIN TROUBLES	88290-2/$3.99
HIP HOP TILL YOU DROP	88291-0/$3.99
HERE COMES THE BRAND NEW ME	89858-2/$3.99
THE SECRET'S OUT	89859-0/$3.99
DADDY'S NOT-SO-LITTLE GIRL	89860-4/$3.99
P.S. FRIENDS FOREVER	89861-2/$3.99
GETTING EVEN WITH THE FLAMINGOES	52273-6/$3.99
THE DUDE OF MY DREAMS	52274-4/$3.99
BACK-TO-SCHOOL COOL	52275-2/$3.99
PICTURE ME FAMOUS	52276-0/$3.99
TWO-FOR-ONE CHRISTMAS FUN	53546-3/$3.99
THE BIG FIX-UP MIX-UP	53547-1/$3.99
TEN WAYS TO WRECK A DATE	53548-X/$3.99
WISH UPON A VCR	53549-8/$3.99
DOUBLES OR NOTHING	56841-8/$3.99
SUGAR AND SPICE ADVICE	56842-6/$3.99
NEVER TRUST A FLAMINGO	56843-4/$3.99
THE TRUTH ABOUT BOYS	00361-5/$3.99
CRAZY ABOUT THE FUTURE	00362-3/$3.99

Available from Minstrel® Books Published by Pocket Books

Simon & Schuster Mail Order Dept. BWB
200 Old Tappan Rd., Old Tappan, N.J. 07675

Please send me the books I have checked above. I am enclosing $_____ (please add $0.75 to cover the postage and handling for each order. Please add appropriate sales tax). Send check or money order--no cash or C.O.D.'s please. Allow up to six weeks for delivery. For purchase over $10.00 you may use VISA: card number, expiration date and customer signature must be included.

Name _____

Address _____

City _____ State/Zip _____

VISA Card # _____ Exp.Date _____

Signature _____

929-19

FULL HOUSE™
Michelle

#1: THE GREAT PET PROJECT 51905-0/$3.50
#2: THE SUPER-DUPER SLEEPOVER PARTY
51906-9/$3.50
#3: MY TWO BEST FRIENDS 52271-X/$3.99
#4: LUCKY, LUCKY DAY 52272-8/$3.50
#5: THE GHOST IN MY CLOSET 53573-0/$3.99
#6: BALLET SURPRISE 53574-9/$3.99
#7: MAJOR LEAGUE TROUBLE 53575-7/$3.99
#8: MY FOURTH-GRADE MESS 53576-5/$3.99
#9: BUNK 3, TEDDY, AND ME 56834-5/$3.99
#10: MY BEST FRIEND IS A MOVIE STAR!
(Super Edition) 56835-3/$3.99
#11: THE BIG TURKEY ESCAPE 56836-1/$3.99
#12: THE SUBSTITUTE TEACHER 00364-X/$3.99
#13: CALLING ALL PLANETS 00365-8/$3.99
#14: I'VE GOT A SECRET 00366-6/$3.99
#15: HOW TO BE COOL 00833-1/$3.99
#16: THE NOT-SO-GREAT OUTDOORS 00835-8/$3.99

A MINSTREL BOOK
Published by Pocket Books

Simon & Schuster Mail Order Dept. BWB
200 Old Tappan Rd., Old Tappan, N.J. 07675

Please send me the books I have checked above. I am enclosing $_____ (please add $0.75 to cover the postage and handling for each order. Please add appropriate sales tax). Send check or money order--no cash or C.O.D.'s please. Allow up to six weeks for delivery. For purchase over $10.00 you may use VISA: card number, expiration date and customer signature must be included.

Name _____
Address _____
City _____ State/Zip _____
VISA Card # _____ Exp. Date _____
Signature _____